The Hug

David Grossman

Artwork by Michal Rovner

Translated from the Hebrew by Stuart Schoffman

Overlook Duckworth
New York · London

This edition first published in the United States and
the United Kingdom in 2013 by Overlook Duckworth,
Peter Mayer Publishers, Inc.

NEW YORK:
The Overlook Press
141 Wooster Street
New York, NY 10012
www.overlookpress.com
For bulk and special sales, please contact sales@overlookny.com,
or write us at the above address

LONDON:
Gerald Duckworth & Co. Ltd.
30 Calvin Street
London E1 6NW
info@duckworth-publishers.co.uk
www.ducknet.co.uk

First published in Israel by Am Oved Publishers, Tel Aviv

Image processing for print: Michael Gordon Studio Ltd. Tel Aviv

Cataloging-in-Publication Data is available from the Library of Congress
A catalogue record for this book is available from the British Library

Manufactured in China
ISBN US: 978-1-4683-0273-8
ISBN UK: 978-0-7156-4587-1

2 4 6 8 10 9 7 5 3 1

"You're sweet," said Ben's mother, as they went
walking in the field in the late afternoon.

"You are so sweet, there's nobody else
like you in the whole wide world!"

"There's really nobody else like me?" asked Ben.

"Certainly not," said his mother.

"You are the one and only!"

They kept walking slowly.

A big flock of storks flew in the sky overhead,
migrating to other lands.

"But why?" asked Ben, and stopped walking.

"Why is there no one else like me in the world?"

"Because everyone is unique and special!" laughed his mother, and sat down on the ground. "Come, sit next to me," she said,

and whistled for their dog, Wonder, to join them.

"I don't want to be the only one like me in the whole world," said Ben.

"Why not? It's wonderful to be so unique and special!" said his mother.

"But then I'm all alone!" said Ben.

"I want there to be someone else like me!"

"You're not alone," said his mother.

"I'm with you, and so is Daddy. Come, sit next
to me," she said, "put your tushie on the ground."

Ben didn't sit down.

His eyes suddenly went wide.

"You mean, there's also nobody else like you in the whole world?"

"No, there isn't," his mother said.

"So you're also alone?"

"Not at all. I have you, and Daddy —"

"But you don't have anyone exactly *exactly* like you?"

"No, I don't," said his mother.

"So you're all alone," said Ben, and sat down next to his mother.

"Don't you feel alone being alone?"

His mother smiled and drew circles on the ground with her finger.

"I'm a little alone, and a little with everyone else,
and it feels good to be a little bit this and a little bit that."

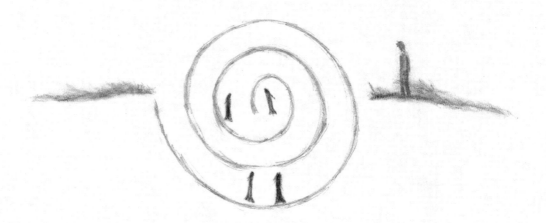

The sun began to go down, and the sky turned almost red.

"I feel alone," Ben said quietly.

"But sweetie," his mother said, "I'm with you!"

"But you're not me."

Then they didn't say anything at all. The air was filled
with a good smell, the smell of soil and grass,

and the buzzing of little flies and bugs that danced and flew all around.

Ben caressed the dog, who was lying next to him: "Also Wonder?"

"Also Wonder what?" asked his mother.

"There's only one like her in the whole world?"

"Yes," said his mother, and she also stroked Wonder's soft fur,

"there's only one Wonder like her in the whole world."

On the ground, near their feet, ants were marching. A long
parade of ants. There were probably a thousand ants. They
all looked the same, like a thousand twin ants. But when
Ben looked closely at them, he saw that one ant was walking
fast, and another ant was walking slowly. And there was one
who was struggling to drag a big leaf,

and another who was only dragging a seed. And there was one,
a little tiny one, who ran back and forth alongside the parade.
Ben thought that maybe she had lost her parents, and was
looking for them.

He asked: "This ant, this one, does she know there's
only one ant like her in the whole world?"

And his mother said: "I have no way of knowing."

Ben thought for a moment, and then said: "Because you're not her?"

"Because I'm not her," said his mother.
The little tiny ant finally returned to the parade, and
walked together with the other ants. Ben thought that
maybe the two big ants walking beside her were her
parents. And he asked,

"So there is only one of everyone in the world?"

"Only one of everyone," said his mother.

"So everyone is alone?"

"Everyone is a little alone, but also together.

They are alone and not alone."

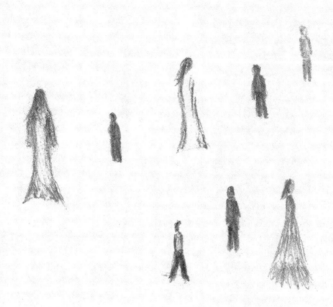

"How can it be both this and that?"

"Here you are, one and only," said his mother, "and I'm also one and only, but if I hug you now, you won't be alone, and I won't be alone."

"So hug me," said Ben, and threw his arms around his mother.

His mother hugged him. She could feel his heart
pounding. Ben also felt his mother's heart.
He hugged her with all his might.

"Now I'm not alone," he thought to himself in the middle
of the hug, "now I'm not alone. Now I'm not alone."

"You see?" whispered his mother.

"This is exactly why hugs were invented."